The Fox and the Grapes

RETOLD BY MARY BERENDES • ILLUSTRATED BY NANCY HARRISON

Distributed by The Child's World®
1980 Lookout Drive • Mankato, MN 56003-1705
800-599-READ • www.childsworld.com

ACKNOWLEDGMENTS
The Child's World®: Mary Berendes, Publishing Director
The Design Lab: Art Direction and Design
Red Line Editorial: Editing

LIBRARY OF CONGRESS CATALOGING-IN-PUBLICATION DATA
Berendes, Mary.
 The fox and the grapes / by Mary Berendes ; illustrated by Nancy Harrison.
    p. cm. — (Aesop's fables)
 Summary: Retells the fable of a frustrated fox that, after many tries to reach a
high bunch of grapes, decides they must be sour anyway.
  ISBN 978-1-60253-525-1 (library bound : alk. paper)
 [1. Fables. 2. Folklore.] I. Harrison, Nancy, 1963- ill. II. Aesop. III. Title. IV. Series.
 PZ8.2.B46925Fox 2010
 398.2—dc22
 [E]   2010009974

Printed in the United States of America in Mankato, Minnesota.
July 2010
F11538

When people cannot get what they want, they sometimes tell themselves that what they want is no good anyway.

One hot day, a fox walked along a path. He noticed a bunch of grapes growing on a tall vine.

The fox licked his lips. The
grapes looked juicy and ripe.
"Mmm," said the fox. "Those
grapes would taste good on
such a hot day."

The fox reached for the grapes,
but they were too high.

He stretched his arms and stood on his tiptoes. He still could not reach the tasty grapes.

The fox walked back a few steps.

He ran forward and jumped—

but he missed the grapes!

The fox tried again. This time, he ran faster and leaped with all his might. But again, he missed the grapes.

Again and again the fox tried.
No matter how hard he ran
or how high he leaped, the
fox couldn't get the grapes.
Finally he gave up.

"I didn't want those old grapes anyway," the fox huffed as he walked away. "I'm sure they are sour!"

AESOP

Aesop was a storyteller who lived more than 2,500 years ago. He lived so long ago, there isn't much information about him. Most people believe Aesop was a slave who lived in the area around the Mediterranean Sea—probably in or near the country of Greece.

Aesop's fables are known in almost every culture in the world, in almost every language. His fables are even *part* of some languages! Some common phrases come from Aesop's fables, such as "sour grapes" and "Never count your chickens before they've hatched."

ABOUT FABLES

Fables are one of the oldest forms of stories. They are often short and funny, and have animals as the main characters. These animals act like people. Often, fables teach the reader a lesson. This is called a *moral*. A moral might teach right from wrong, or show how to act in good, kind ways. A moral might show what happens when someone makes a poor decision. Fables teach us how to live wisely.

Mary Berendes has authored dozens of books for children, including nature titles as well as books about countries and holidays. She loves to collect antique books and has some that are almost 200 years old. Mary lives in Minnesota.

Nancy Harrison was born and raised in Montreal. She has worked as an art director, creative director, and advertising executive with clients all over the world. After relocating to Philadelphia, she began working as a freelance illustrator. Nancy's work has been published in dozens of magazines and over 30 children's books. Nancy currently lives in Vermont.